THROW A KISS, HARRY

STORY AND PICTURES BY
Mary Chalmers

HARPER & ROW, PUBLISHERS
NEW YORK, EVANSTON, AND LONDON

TO BOATS

One morning Harry went for a walk
with his mother.

He found a turtle. "Hello, turtle," he said. "I'll pick you a flower."

6

"Harry, leave the turtle alone, and come along," said his mother.

8

His mother stopped to talk to a friend

and Harry wandered off by himself.

He saw a house.

He climbed to the top of a tree and
from there to the roof of the house. It
was very high.

"Oh, my goodness!" cried his mother. "Harry! Come down from there this instant!" But the truth of the matter was that Harry didn't know how to come down.

Someone called the Fire Department
and they sent their best hook and ladder truck.

They put up a great, long ladder an
a fireman carried Harry safely down.

"There," said Harry's mother. "You see what happens when you go wandering off by yourself? Now come along home."

18

But Harry had had a lovely time be-
ing rescued. He did not want to go
home. He waved to the fireman and
the fireman waved back.

Harry kept on waving.
Finally his mother said,

"Well, why don't you throw a kiss
to the fireman?"

"Harry, throw a kiss to the fireman.
Go on now, be a good boy."

"Oh dear! Any other time he would."

"Throw a kiss or I'll tell your father to give you a spanking when you get home."

"Well, he isn't behaving today," said
Harry's mother.

"Harry, come on home now," she said.